LITTLE LUNCH TRUCK

Charles Beyl

Feiwel and Friends | New York

Little Lunch Truck is dedicated to my children and grandchildren. I am forever grateful for their inspiration and love.

A FEIWEL AND FRIENDS BOOK
An imprint of Macmillan Publishing Group, LLC
120 Broadway, New York, NY 10271
mackids.com

Library of Congress Cataloging-in-Publication Data is available.

First edition, 2021
Book design by Mallory Grigg and Trisha Previte
Printed in China by RR Donnelley Asia Printing Solutions Ltd.,
Dongguan City, Guangdong Province
Feiwel and Friends logo designed by Filomena Tuosto

The artwork was created with pencil, paper, and Adobe Photoshop.

ISBN 978-1-250-25577-8 (hardcover)
10 9 8 7 6 5 4 3 2 1

LITTLE
LUNCH

Chef Nina and Little Lunch Truck
drive to work together every day.

They make stops all around town.

The Library

The Town Square

The Hospital

The Fire Station

The Park

Little Lunch Truck shines with pride as people line up for Chef Nina's sandwiches, chili, tacos, salads, fruit smoothies, fresh homemade guacamole, and especially her famous Sweet Tater Fries.

Today is a big day for Little Lunch Truck.
Chef Nina is driving to the construction site.

The construction site
is dusty, dirty, busy . . .

and loud.

And **EXCITING!**

All those great big construction trucks!
Little Lunch Truck can't wait to meet them.

As Chef Nina drives quietly toward the construction site, Little Lunch Truck's pots and pans shiver.

His wheels grip the pavement and he begins to worry—just a little bit. "Will the Big Trucks like me? Will they even notice me?"

Little Lunch Truck drives by Bulldozer pushing dirt, and Bulldozer stops pushing.

Little Lunch Truck
drives by Cement Mixer
pouring a foundation, and
Cement Mixer stops mixing.

Little Lunch Truck drives by
Backhoe digging a hole,
and Backhoe stops digging.

Watch out!
Don't get too close!

Little Lunch Truck drives by Skid Loader carrying sacks of concrete mix, and Skid Loader stops carrying.

Little Lunch Truck drives by Front End Loader and Dump Truck shoveling and moving earth away, and they stop shoveling and moving.

Little Lunch Truck drives by Big Crane lifting
massive steel beams, and Big Crane stops lifting.

All the construction trucks gather around
Little Lunch Truck. "Why are they looking at us?"
Little Lunch Truck wonders.
"Are they mad that we interrupted their work?"

Chef Nina opens the big window
and calls out,
        "Time for lunch!"

At first, it is so quiet that you could hear the birds singing.

But suddenly, the construction workers shout, "Hurray!" They're very happy to eat Chef Nina's tacos, sandwiches, chili, and salad—and of course, her special Sweet Tater Fries!

When all the workers have bought their food, Little Lunch Truck and Chef Nina pack up and drive away. All the construction trucks are ready to get back to lifting and carrying and moving and digging. "Come back tomorrow, little buddy!" calls Bulldozer.

"Beep beep! We'll be back for sure!" says Little Lunch Truck.

What a great day!